For Wendy Cooling, Polar Explorer.
Warm wishes —T. M.

For Bump,
with love —G. P-R.

Text copyright © 2007 by Tony Mitton
Illustrations copyright © 2007 by Guy Parker-Rees
First published as *Perky Little Penguins* in 2007 by Orchard Books in Great Britain

Published in the United States of America in 2007 by Walker Publishing Company, Inc.
Distributed to the trade by Holtzbrinck Publishers

For information about permission to reproduce selections from this book, write to
Permissions, Walker & Company, 104 Fifth Avenue, New York, New York 10011

Library of Congress Cataloging-in-Publication Data
Mitton, Tony.
[Perky little penguins]
Playful little penguins / by Tony Mitton ; illustrated by Guy Parker-Rees.
p.   cm.
Summary: While enjoying a full day of their favorite activities,
a group of young penguins helps a baby seal that has been separated from her mother.
ISBN-13: 978-0-8027-9710-0 • ISBN-10: 0-8027-9710-5 (hardcover)
[1. Penguins—Fiction. 2. Play—Fiction. 3. Day—Fiction. 4. Seals (Animals)—Fiction.
5. Animals—Infancy—Fiction. 6. Stories in rhyme.] I. Parker-Rees, Guy, ill. II. Title.
PZ8.3.M685Pla 2007   [E]—dc22   2007006683

Visit Walker & Company's Web site at www.walkeryoungreaders.com

Printed in China
2 4 6 8 10 9 7 5 3 1

PLAYFUL
LITTLE
PENGUINS

Tony Mitton

illustrations by
Guy Parker-Rees

Walker & Company
New York

Playful little penguins

coming out today,

Playful little penguins
in the wintry weather—

that's how penguins like to move,
waddling 'round together.

Playful little penguins make a shiny slide. "Wheeeee!" shout the penguins. "What a silly ride!"

Playful little penguins,
as they jump around,
make a chirpy, squeaky noise—
what a funny sound!

Playful little penguins
are hungry for their lunch—

off they go to look for it,
in a busy bunch.

Playful little penguins
in the wintry weather—
that's how penguins look for lunch,
leaping out together.

Eager little penguins
jumping in the sea,

"yay!" shout the penguins.
"That's the place to be!"

They swirl around,

they whirl around,

splashy, sploshy, splish.

They curl around,

they twirl around,

catching tasty fish.

Playful little penguins in the wintry weather—
that's how penguins like to eat,
swimming 'round together.

But what's this on the ice floe?
A little ball of fur?
A sobbing baby seal pup!
So what's wrong with her?

"Poor little seal pup,
what could be so bad?
You're looking really frightened.
Why are you so sad?"

"My mama saw some fish swim by and dove into the sea.
The ice floe we were resting on went drifting off with me!"

All the friendly penguins try to cheer her up.

Soon she seems happy, a smiling little pup!

The penguins do a silly dance—
how they jump and wiggle!

Now the little seal pup
begins to grin and giggle.

Playful little penguins
in the wintry weather—
that's how penguins have their fun,
jumping 'round together.

But what's that in the water?
Help, it's coming near!
It's speedy and it's shadowy.
It fills them all with fear.

It's heading straight toward them.
It leaps up on the floe . . .

Look, it's Seal Pup's mother. See? We told you so.

Seal Pup calls to Mama
with a squeaky little yelp.

Then Mama thanks the penguins
for their kindness and their help.

Mama Seal takes Seal Pup.

They slowly swim away.

Then the penguins realize it's time to end their day.

Playful little penguins,
how sleepily they go—
waddling and **yawning**,
through the ice and snow.

Home they go together,
back to Mom and Dad.
They tell them all the things they've done
and all the fun they've had.

Sleepy little penguins
in a happy huddle—
that's how penguins like to rest,

in a cozy cuddle!